D1000248

Oscar Owl Gives a Hoot About Color

by: Camille A. Frazer

Artist: Kalin_zee

Camille A. Frazer
PO Box 880925
Port St. Lucie, FL 34988

ISBN: 978-0-9995230-1-8
ISBN: 978-0-9995230-2-5

Oscar Owl
Perched in a tree
Offers his thoughts
On race and equality

The world is full of people
Black, brown and white

Who need to come together

Who need to unite

Each is beautiful

No matter the color of their skin

Each is beautiful
No matter the color
they were given

Think of the crayons
In your box

Each paints a color
Unique and wondrous

No color is better
Than the other

They make beautiful pictures
When painted together

So do people
When we love each other

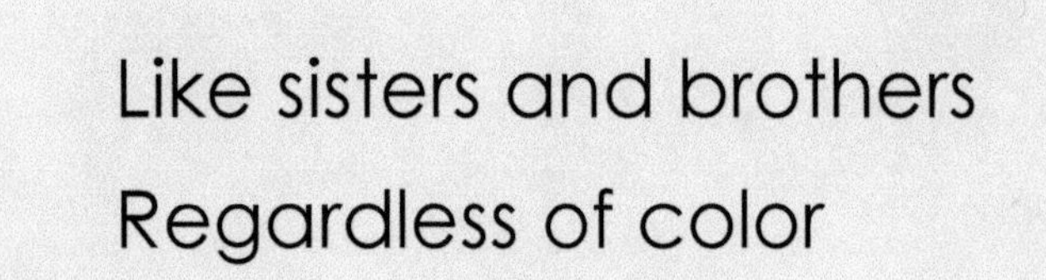

Like sisters and brothers
Regardless of color

Always remember each person
Is precious and unique

Together, we color the world
With exactly what it needs

When you see someone being
unkind to another

Because of the color of their skin

Tell them we are all equal
And that together we all win.

This is how

Love wins over hate

When we come together

For the world we seek to create

Create a world of
Love, Respect and Equality.

About the Author

Camille A. Frazer is a Child Advocate Attorney. She was born in Jamaica and currently resides in Florida, where she has ardently advocated for the well-being of children since 2005.

CPSIA information can be obtained
at www.ICGtesting.com
Printed in the USA
BVHW020215260820
587332BV00022B/121

9 780999 523032